The Very
Lazy Ladybug

tiger tales

5 River Road, Suite 128, Wilton, CT 06897
This edition published in the United States 2019
First paperback edition (978-1-58925-379-7) published 2003
First hardcover edition (978-1-58925-007-9) published 2001
Originally published in Great Britain 1999
by Little Tiger Press Ltd.
Text copyright © 1999 Isobel Finn
Illustrations copyright © 1999 Jack Tickle
ISBN-13: 978-1-68010-139-3
ISBN-10: 1-68010-139-0
Printed in China
LTP/1400/2378/0818
All rights reserved
10 9 8 7 6 5 4 3 2 1

For more insight and activities, visit us at www.tigertalesbooks.com

The Very Lazy Ladybug

by
Isobel Finn

Illustrated by
Jack Tickle

tiger tales

This is the story of
a very lazy ladybug.

She liked to sleep all day . . .

and all night.

Because she slept
all day and all night,
this lazy ladybug didn't
know how to fly.

One day, the lazy ladybug wanted to sleep somewhere else. But what could she do if she couldn't fly?

Then the lazy ladybug had a very good idea.

when a kangaroo bounded by . . .

"I can't sleep in here!"
cried the lazy ladybug.
"It's too bumpy."

So when a tiger padded by . . .